LOVE NOTES

Single Hearts Affairs

LOVE NOTES

Single Hearts Affairs

TWINKLE ZAMAN

Copyright © 2021 by Twinkle Zaman.

All rights reserved. No part of this book may be reproduced in any form or by any electronic or mechanical means, including information storage and retrieval systems, without permission in writing from the publisher, except by reviewers, who may quote brief passages in a review.

ISBN: 978-1-956074-60-4 (Paperback Edition)
ISBN: 978-1-956074-61-1 (Hardcover Edition)
ISBN: 978-1-956074-59-8 (E-book Edition)

Book Ordering Information

Phone Number: 315 288-7939 ext. 1000 or 347-901-4920
Email: info@globalsummithouse.com
Global Summit House
www.globalsummithouse.com

Printed in the United States of America

For the one holding this book
Even when you don't see it and they don't see it
Always know in this world you are enough

INTRO

Gate C6 is now boarding group B. I heard it over the intercom! It was always like, 'what the hell am I doing and what's the point of all this' and 'so what's going to happen next after this?' My mind was always thinking ahead, even though I hadn't even lived the next two days of my life yet.

Don't get me wrong, I'm always excited...the thrill of a new city, live music, feeling good in a cute outfit, adventures with my best friend who was always up for whatever, exploring the culture of the place and, sometimes, no culture at all! It's always an adventure, from fancy hotels to roadside dumps. I wouldn't trade one for the other.

The highs of all these moments are insane! It's this overwhelming feeling that makes me believe I can conquer the world. Nothing feels above me, but on the other hand, the lows are low. I'm completely defeated. Days when I can't take a full breath or when it feels like a rock is sitting on my chest.

The money I'd lose, the days off work I'd have to take, the lies I'd have to tell family and friends. It's a sensation that only I understand. I firmly believe that the journey has shaped me into the woman I am today.

I've learned a lot. I know it sounds crazy, but he has been, a huge part of my evolution. How did he lead me to myself? I feel like I've been studying him for years. I mean that in a way that makes me realize what kind of person he is. I've never had that feeling about anyone before. It's very intriguing. His presence and aura always make me feel powerful... yet powerless in his presence. The irony is a different kind of pain, for someone not seeing who they've helped you become and the sense of not feeling enough. I don't think people will ever understand these things because they simply don't know. It's a difficult concept to explain, and it's difficult for me to grasp at times. My life has changed for the better as he has guided me in becoming who I am. I'm much stronger, more fearless, and don't mind standing up for what I believe in.

I wish every woman could experience those emotions. Not only love for another, but ultimately love for oneself, knowing one's worth and sharing one's power with the world. There's something special about someone who can bring that out of you, but it's also painful when they can't see it in you. And so here I am! I wrote this book for all my ladies who need to be reminded of how special they are, especially if they have forgotten who they are. I hope you find yourself; you don't need a man to do so, but a hot stud always adds a little spice! Be crazy, chase the man, chase the dream, and I hope you know you are always enough, even when it doesn't feel like it!

Twinkle

[Believe]

accept (something) as true;
feel sure of the truth of.

Woman Within

There are many adventures in life, but none compare to the adventure of discovering yourself. There's something magical about becoming yourself and fully accepting your flaws. I was just following the crowd a decade ago, doing what I thought I needed to do to fit in. Not only was I failing to please others, but I was also failing to please myself. I never felt like I belonged, I was never pretty enough, and most days I didn't feel good enough. What I've learned about myself on this journey is my worth, self-respect, and, most importantly, how to love myself. I've discovered a fiery, passionate, and wild side of myself that I had no idea existed. While we were getting ready one day, a friend of mine asked me, "Do you feel like a woman?" We were about 25 or 26 years old at the time. My answer was yes, but I took a moment to consider what that meant to me. I've struggled my entire life with a lack of confidence, being shy, and constantly feeling judged. As I've progressed on this path of self-discovery, I've gradually gained confidence; the shyness comes and goes, and I honestly don't care what others think of me as long as I'm happy with what I'm doing. I don't think we should ever stop evolving. These short stories you are about to read are the result of my journey to find myself. Sure, I talk a lot about love, but I've also learned to love myself. Moments of weakness, interactions with people from various walks of life, putting myself in new situations and learning to navigate, and, most importantly, always following my wild heart. If you let it, life is a wild and beautiful ride. I've discovered that no matter what my mind tells me to do, I'm always led by my heart. Following my heart brought me to myself. I love who I've become, who I'll continue to become, and all the adventures I haven't yet had. The journey to oneself is never complete. I will continue to dream, continue to grow, and continue to search for my purpose. Be the kind of woman that leaves marks everywhere she goes and on everything she touches.

Identity

We all lose ourselves in time
To love, to lust whatever maybe the cost
Doesn't take long before we don't know who we are
Don't we all say it won't ever get that far
I found my truest self in you
I met the woman in me I never knew
Such an exhilarating feeling to become
More than I could ever imagine and then some
Who I am today I feel I owe it all to you
For being the man you are it's true
I could've never imagined this version of me
Darling, you are my identity

The things you've shown me you don't know

The places now this body, mind and soul goes
Show me the way to myself

The secret path when there's no one else

The passion that exists within me

All I have to do is think of your touch to set myself free

Everyone tells me you can't have a man like that
What if you can
What if you can have someone who makes you feel good
Someone who sets your soul on fire
Someone who brings out a part of you you've never met before
What if you can have it all
Why do we believe as woman it's one or the other
Who made us believe we should settle for less than we deserve

One in a million

In a world where there's beauty all around
I'm glad you saw me at my worst
Didn't know then that it was the universe I had to trust
Maybe I'm not but I'm glad I could pull you in with my eyes
Maybe I'm crazy
Maybe it's lies
But sometimes I do feel like one in a million who caught your eyes
One in a million who got to fall into the night
The one in a million who believes she just might
Be one in a million for a second in time

Skin, heart & bones

I pour the wine one more time
I may not have you but my heart calls you mine
I ain't ever met somebody who compliments my skin, heart and bones
I know I know I'm good even though I spend my days alone
I look in the mirror and see my reflection
For once I love me
My skin, heart and bones

Ball

I know I'm judged for becoming me
I know they hate the way you've gotten to me
I love that you opened my eyes
To let myself explore
To take every chance behind every door
To never let a man tear me down
To be solid and hold my ground
Evil eyes I see them all
Welcome to adulthood it's a ball

Reflection

Law of attraction
I believe it
When I see me, I see you, I live for it
Every inch every bit
You are my reflection
A golden attraction
An energy from the universe
It's us
Perfect reflection

Foundation

What am I building on I ask myself
Am I crazy to build this dream off of somebody else
Cause when you got me so high
I'm a go-getter reaching for the sky
When you make me cry
I don't even know my purpose anymore
I ask myself why
This foundation has never been stable
Somehow I got here and I still believe with you I'm able
I just hope it doesn't ever completely shatter
I've spent almost a decade here and it all truly matters

Saving Time

They think I'm probably wasting time
It's been nothing but teardrops and good times
We're aging like fine wine
Like fine wine
Baby, I think we're saving time
Lines coming in on our faces
This life ain't a race
We're just saving time
Another bottle
Pass the wine

Old Soul

Beyond my years
Chasing you
Gray hairs coming in
I'm wise but when it comes to you
Wisdom is hard to find
An old soul that just won't quit
Cause I know these two old souls just happen to fit

Mirror

When I look at you I feel beautiful in this skin
when I look at you even when the worlds against me
I feel like I always win
when I look at you I don't think twice
About those doubts I have
the demons, the lies

You are my mirror, mirror
I look at you I see everything so clear
and sometimes it may be foggy
they say I'm delusional
and it may be illusional

Sometimes when we come face to face it's a fight
I guess it's not always the right angle
ain't the right light
then there I go feelin so glamorous
and you, you being so amorous

Smoke and mirrors
it's a fight
day and night
can't look once
gotta look twice
cause it's just me standing
in the mirror

Young Girls

We don't know better when we've just stepped out
The love we think is love or what it's all about
We're just young
Young young girls
Trying to get the man
Trying to fit into the world
The things we do to fit the mold
Just to have someone's touch someone to hold
We don't listen til we're grown
And now we think we know
we still don't know
Cause now we're judging the young girls

Woman In Me

The same day I called my friend driving down Patton Rd racing cars
Telling you I'll be there soon I'm not that far
I told her I just want him to finally see the woman I am, the woman in me
And the next day you said to me for the first time you saw me and saw the woman in me
Took so long for me to be myself in front of you
Cause all these years I've been getting ready to be this woman
The woman in me that I saved for you

Road To You

Where am I going
I've never been
It's a lose or a win
Some kinda midnight sin
Road to you is wild and free
Road to you is a hidden gem

Body

I never knew my body before you
I was 21 without a clue
The one I was with was selfish and useless
You knew the way under every cotton dress
You touch my body like nobody
You've made my body into what it is

Changed

People say I've changed
I agree
I'm finally becoming me
Finally seeing all the colors of the world
It hurts to grow
Hurts to see the unkind
So I just learned to stay to myself
Flourish in the goodness that I find

When you're young you just wanna believe that at
any minute anything can happen
then you start getting older and the more hurt and the
more
pain you experience the less you believe
don't you wish we could just hold onto that
innocent magic forever

I feel like I can only hold my happiness for so long
Before I know it I'm right back where I started and it's gone

Time Will Tell

Time will tell
So they say, but I can't wait another day
I wanna be where I see you in my head
Already over this blue and into the red
Time will tell yeah, time will tell
Until then I'll be sitting here in this burning hell

A Lover

I'm a lover
Maybe a little love sick
I love the magic but not the tricks
I like you here
Not when you disappear

I find glory in making a story
One that we look back on and smile
Or fall down and cry for a while
Maybe I'm an addict from one extreme to another
Just a little crazy but a wild lover

Pain Pill

I've got so many problems, none that I can fix
Then my world is all shaken up with you in the mix
I feel invisible in this world
Invisible in your eyes
Can you feel the water when I cry
You're like a pain pill
It's only a temporary high
You're like a pain pill
With you, I feel like I can fly

Hurting Alone

Everybody thinks what they think
I guess just as much as I tell them
I mostly say the good things
I don't want them to hate him

It's hard hurting alone
It's hard crying alone
It's hard sleeping alone
Even if I say it, no I don't enjoy being on my own
Mostly everything's alright
But there's nothing like hurting alone
When I'm supposed to wake up at the end of the night

Everybody's got their own lives now
So I don't bother them with mine
I'll figure out mine in time

I guess I've bloomed since the days I remember
I used to have a lover but we lost it way
before *2015* of December
I never looked at him the way I look at you
And when I look around I wonder do you even have a clue

If you find me lost in a daze
I'm just dreaming about the days
The days that have not yet come

Talk Around The Table

Yeah I'm the talk around the table when I ain't even there
Why does it matter, why do they care
Yeah there's more to me than meets the eye
Someone's always curious they wanna know the truth in between the lines

People get to talking over beer and wine
Tell your own stories why does it gotta be mine
Someone's always out there ready to expose
what they think but they never really know
Don't make me the talk around the table

Confident

I've thought a lot about you today
Just like how I start and end my days
I think about what I'd tell you
Until it's time to forget
I get the tingle at the tip of my fingertips
I just can't make the right words come out of these lips

I find it so funny confident is what you made me
But anything but confidence is what you see
The words never come out the way they should
I never say it in person the way I picture I would
I don't have the nerve to break this wall
Because if you don't catch me I don't wanna fall

Midnight Blues

She can put on her lipstick
Paint her face with a flawless smile
Make a pointless conversation to pass time with a stranger for a while
She can turn up the music that takes her through the highs and lows
How she's really feeling inside nobody knows

She may be missing him deep inside
She knows everyone's tired of hearing about her crazy ride
She knows no one will get it until they walk in her worn-out shoes
She's walking with a smile until she comes back home to her midnight blues

Girls Like Me

Girls like me we don't go around
We're the last ones saved the last ones found
I'm starting to miss a goodnight kiss
I'm starting to want things I used to diss
Walls are closing in when I'm laying in my bed
I'm seeing him go around in my head

I want somebody good and well
Not someone to just kiss and tell
I'm starting to miss arms to fall into
I'm starting to want the things, just for us two

Rare One

I can bring myself to show up with a smile
have a drink or two
Listen to the music that tracks my mind back to you
I can hold myself up enough until I'm alone
I can walk with confidence when I'm falling apart
They think it's freedom that I own

I'm a soft smile in a small town cafe
I don't open the book often but if you're going through a hard time
I'll pray
I'm the only car driving on a rainy night
When the winds pushing me left I'll most likely go right
I'm a rare one

Map

You are the map that I follow
Life's had me lost but you've been my arrow
Some days I don't know
Where you take me, I go

Of course, I didn't buy *$200* worth of lingerie to please you,
obviously to roll around in my own bed
I should know this by now

Letter To Myself

Sweet girl
I'm telling you
You're blind now
But what they say is true
Love is a game, you'll always lose
Rarely do you win
So drink up now, spend the money on the booze
Run if you have to
Hold him close
Just know in your heart this is how the game goes
It's not you, it's always them
I can't break my habit
I'll always want him

Love Story

She had a love story in her mind
She wanted to find her kind
Someone who lit her heart in the dark
She was out, out to find that spark

No Clue

I wish I could tell you who I really am
Or you could just find out if that's part of the plan
You think I don't measure up to your high
Well, well, well you don't know the truth but I never told a lie
Keep belittling me the way you do
I think it's funny, you have no clue

I drink coffee for breakfast and eat my feelings for dinner

Everybody Else

I don't think like everybody else
I don't feel like everybody else
I don't have a thousand places to run when you ignore me
I'm a one-man kinda girl
The way I'll always be

I'll sit in my lonely cause sometimes that's okay
I get it
Life won't always go my way
Sure it'd be easy to have someone be my comfort
I'd rather be alone and endure the hurt

I don't love like everybody else
I don't dream like everybody else
I'll never be like them
I'm no better but I ain't like everybody else

My Friends

My friends
They would say she hides away the best there is to her
She's careful because she wants you so bad
She doesn't wanna drive you mad
My friends
They would say she's a dreamer just like you
We don't know why she doesn't tell you
My friends
They would say she's crazy and quirky all in one
Give her a couple of chances she won't be long
My friends
They tell me to say all this
I so badly want to, one day I will but right now it's just a wish

Loveless Girl

She ain't bad looking on days when she pulls herself together
She doesn't wanna be picky but she just wants better
She's a warm smile with a fragile heart
She keeps it together even when she's falling apart
They say why are you loveless girl
You give the world
The world just ain't giving back to her
She's a loveless mess
Maybe some of us are meant to be loved less

I bought the dress, even though I had nowhere to wear it to. I dreamed about someday wearing it for him.

Debt To Myself

Call up a hotel the night before
To book a room with a dumpster view
I've also slept half a night in a crowded parking lot for you
Tell me you like my curls
Maybe my dress, but my lips will never tell you the crazy mess
I leave behind when I come to love on you
Maybe I'm waiting to pay a bill after I get back in town
Maybe it's worth it when for a second you turn my life sadness around
And you'll never know how I drown
In debt to myself
And I'll never talk about money
I'll keep saving my pennies and dimes
In debt to myself
The miles that never equal the time

Worry In My Head

I'm a warm coffee in my hand
When the world is feeling extra cold
I'm a fast lane driver when you're flying away
You don't know but the hope of you carries me through
Because of you
All the worry in my head
It doesn't matter what they said
The devil can't fight me tonight in bed
All the worry in my head
I'm crazy it's been said
Because of you sometimes I can rest all the worry in my head

He made me want to chase myself
not fancy cars or designer bags but me
he was that kinda man
that really made me want the simple things
like a cup of coffee and the smell of sweet rain

Remember Me

Most forget themselves when they claim to find the one
Everything they once knew in a blink is gone
The sad and true story I've seen time and time again
It's the way we are as a woman
The way we give it all up for men
With you, I've come to find
I'll tell you forever you're one of a kind
When I thought I was losing myself with him
I met you and met myself again
When most seem to forget themselves
You helped me remember me again
Thanks to you I am me, this woman

27

27, I'm 27
Where did the time go
I'm hearing the clock tick
Wasn't long ago
Sometimes I feel like I've got nothing to show
I feel like I should have something to call my own
I'm still hanging on sleeping alone
The hope is still there somehow we gotta believe
Sometimes I feel just like you this dream is just a tease
I wanna believe that we live to have something great
Why are we all rushing
When is it really too late
I'm only 27

Chasing Love

Oh, love...the one thing that keeps the world turning. We all have the desire to be wanted, accepted, and desired. You'd think that because it's so human, it wouldn't be as complicated as we all make it out to be, but it is. There are numerous types of love and reasons why we love who we do. It's also worth noting that what you want when you're young is very different from what you want when you're older. I believe that some of the best people we fall for are those who appear out of nowhere in our lives. My journey has taught me a lot about myself and the type of man I want in my life. My family and friends have always thought that the kind of love I yearn for is unattainable. I don't believe so. I refuse to accept anything less. When I imagine the man of my dreams, I envision someone who inspires me to live my life authentically, someone who shares my values, someone who dreams as big as me, and, most importantly, someone who can lead. When I think of my ideal man, I envision someone who is also my soulmate. Even when he doesn't speak, I can hear his heartbeat when I sit next to him. This kind of connection is surreal, but it's also very real and raw! That's the kind of depth I'm looking for in a relationship. It's not completely out of reach, in my opinion. I believe that if you ever get close to it, you should do whatever it takes to keep chasing that feeling! I never want to feel at ease in love. I want our life together to be liberating, adventurous, intense, passionate, and to keep us on our toes! On sad days, I want my lover to love away from my sadness, and on happy days, I want him to dance with me. You're probably wondering what kind of movies this girl has been watching. There are none! This is something, I believe to be true. The small taste I've had here and there tells me and makes me believe that I can have love, that it is love. Love is more than just a relationship and a way to make ends meet. In some ways, I'm a little traditional, and I still believe that true love is a sacred thing. I just don't want the man; I guess I want the craziness as well!

Fire In Your Eyes

The sun is shining so bright
This must be the first time we're sitting in daylight
Much hasn't changed I still feel it burning
When I look at you
Baby I see fire burning in your eyes
Do you realize
No, you can't hide
The flames
Baby I see fire burning in your eyes

Wild Is

Wild is the way I crave your touch
Wild is how I see through your eyes
Wild is the way your body speaks
Wild is your voice that hits every note
Wild is how this goes
Wild is how I feel
Wild wild wild
Wild is me forever lost in you

Life Knows

Life knows I needed you to show me
Life knows I needed you to know me
Life knows all my flaws
And after all, life knows
I need you still to catch a full breath
Life knows it got me hanging on to you cause if it ain't you, I haven't met him yet
Life knows, I must need you some days more than I need me

There's no torture quite like
having exactly what you want in front of you
And not having it

Underneath it all

They can't see me from the outside
What's going on inside
My head in the clouds, my bodies screaming loud
It's a burning fire underneath it all
Waiting for you
My clothes are ready to fall
Underneath it all
I'm screaming your name
It's burning fire
My body's ready to get high on that wire
Underneath it all

On Paper

I've got some nerve to say what I won't to you on this paper
Cause right now it's dark and it's in the middle of the night
Writing to you is my way to the light
I'll write I love you
I may even picture what you may look like when I say it
Cause on paper I've got the nerve
On paper, I can pour another glass pour out all the hurt
On paper, I'll say it how it goes
These papers, got my heart and soul

Shameless

You know I'll write you twice
Even if you don't reply
I still hit send
Some call it crazy, but for me baby
I think you know it's just me showing some affection
It's an uncontrollable addiction
I can't help it
I think you kinda get it
Even if sometimes I regret it
I don't care cause you've seen me naked and now I just can't fake it
Maybe it's I'm shameless

Through a mirror

Wake up baby wake up
Do you see me
Do you ever look in the mirror
I've been standing here
For all these years
I've a believer, a hard believer
Why my heart hasn't turned away
And why you still haven't found the one to say
I do because I'm thinking maybe It's supposed to be me and you

Baby Blue

When I'm thinking about you
On a rainy Sunday, I'm feeling everything
I'm feeling baby blue
Sitting here daydreaming about you
Baby, baby I'm tired of feeling blue
All I want is you
Baby, baby I'm tired of feeling blue

You

If I've ever dreamed of a love it would be you
If I ever saw love it would be you
If they asked what love looked like to me it would be you
My forever definition of love is you

Palms

Since the day I met you
You've had me in your palm
You've seen me crazy, the times I couldn't keep calm
I just wanna know the future
Is it written in your hand
I just wanna understand
Can I read the lines
See what's behind
Cause you've got my world in your palms
Baby, baby I can't move on
Can I see how many children you and I will have
Can I see if this love will ever be enough
Baby, baby you've had me in the center of your palms

Dancin in your dreams

I hope when you close your eyes at night
I hope you see the stars and twinkling lights
Right above the ocean
I hope the bed starts rockin you in slow motion
As I'm dancin in your dreams
I told you I'm crazy but baby it gets crazier than it seems
As I'm dancin in your dreams

It seems I'm always chasing the next moment
the next place, the next city, the next adventure
I have a hard time just being
I'm not sure I'll ever be present where I am
not until I'm there with you
and my heart can finally beat steady

Sugar Rush

I can't explain the way this feels
My heart racing faster than these wheels
It's a high
They can't get why
You're my sugar rush
Just one touch
Just one taste
Sweet like sugar
Got me excited
I can't hide it
Give me a sugar rush

Love is...

Love is when you treat me like that and I say it's okay
Love is when you walk away
And I run as fast as I can across a busy street
Or a stairway alley behind an old theatre in the dark
Love is when you're running away and I'm still chasing the sparks
Love is baby love

He was always so respectful
That's one thing I can always say
Never forceful and always comforting
Sometimes when he feared I was nervous
He would even ask if I just wanted to just sit and talk
I've always known he was a good one

Irony

You tell me it's your first time seeing me this way
To that, I don't know what to say
What an irony if you could see
So much to explore a different part of me
I've held back through the years
Had my reservations, ghosts, and fears
Maybe I've hurt what was meant to be
Oh baby if you could see the irony

Confession

I never told you this
I couldn't pass up the kiss
It never felt wrong
Am I wrong I cheated
Let my emotions always lead
I never thought of him
Only my needs
I was gone long before you

Vineyard

You compare her to me
Sometimes it hurts my feelings
So I went and I looked her up
She's a blonde beauty
As I scrolled through I realize she's a lot like me
I even saw once we were at the same vineyard at the same time
The day I left to go meet you after wine
What a small world
What a small town
Crazy how everyone is just going around and around

Love

Why do we need it
If only it always hurts
The magical sparks when it always starts
Addiction at its finest taking us through the highs and the lows
Does it ever go any different
Do we know
Love you always hurt
Is pleasure always pain
Does the sunshine always turn to rain

Imprint

In empty halls of hotels I've pondered
After late-night kisses been lost and wondered
Why I keep running up and down these halls
After the door closes behind me
There's never a call
As I walk down old vintage carpets red and blue
My body's only left with imprints of you
From every edge of me you touched
The way you make the blood in my body rush
I'm walking with your imprints down this hall
Hoping the door opens, call baby call

Your Blood and Mine

You talk like poetry
Perfect in every way
Catch me smiling, looking away
Hiding my face under the sheets
Life without you would be hard to beat
We talk about it but only as jokes
In my mind, you know the words soak
Let's mix your blood and mine
We keep making the same baby jokes time after time
I'm ready to write the future
With your blood and mine

Seven Years

It only took seven years for me to spill the beans
To finally say almost everything I mean
I still can't say I love you
And with these feeling, there's no healing
I've tried to say it ain't so
I've told my heart to let those words go
I don't know a lot but I know after seven years
If this is how I still feel then this must not be a fluke
This shit must be real

My Eyes Say It

When I look at you
The world stops
My mouth forgets how to work
You say you can't tell what I'm thinking
Well I love you
My eyes say it

I've been working up the nerve to say what I wanna say

Air

I start getting the happy kinda nervous
Something starts tingling in my hands and feet
Something makes me wanna do the happy dance and smell the roses
I would say it's something in the water
It's just you, It's you in the air

To The Man of My Dreams

I'd make you breakfast not cause I have to but cause I want to

I'd rub your back after a long work day

Then of course I'd let you have your way

I want lazy rainy days where we are lost in each other's eyes

I bet ten years in if you said I was pretty I would still look away shy

I'd cry in your arms every night cause I'd feel lucky to lay with you

I'd tell you over and over again to make sure you always knew I was true

I'd listen to you and all of your dreams

I'd wanna be your equal, not your other half as crazy as it seems

I'd be excited to go to sleep just to wake up and give you coffee breath kisses

We would never be the kind to drink out of mugs that read Mr. and Mrs.

It'd be the honor of my life to serve as your wife

And to be one

I'd still wanna be seventy and make out the way we do now

Good Guy

I see you trying hard to take me out to grab a drink
I know I should go but I don't wanna catch feelings, that's just how I think
I see you telling me nice things that should make me smile
It will for a minute but the thought of him will cloud my mind in a little while

I see the good guys who try so hard
And it's so sad they never get far
It's not them it's me
I've been into the bad ones low key
I see the good guys
But it's me and I don't know why
I know I should want a good guy

I'm so ready to be treated well
It's hard to break bad habits when you're under a spell
I know I should give my time to the ones who wanna spend theirs with mine
I tell them I'm busy, I'm fine

I see the good guys who try so hard
And it's so sad they never get far
It's not them it's me
I've been into the bad ones low key
I see the good guys
But it's me and I don't know why
I know I should want a good guy

Allure Me

When we're in the same place I can't resist
I need space
I feel you when you don't touch me
One more drink, then I'm free

The way you look at me
I can't stand here, you allure me
A magnetic pull without a string
Let's go, I wanna see what you can bring
Allure me

Separate ways, same place
Drunk on you
Love daze

The way you look at me
I can't stand here, you allure me
A magnetic pull without a string
Let's go, I wanna see what you can bring
Allure me

Is It Like You

I never felt love
The way you see in the movies
I've always cared so much but never felt enough
Oh baby I've never felt love

But is it like you
Is it when we're finally alone and my heart starts racing
Is it when I want to you so bad I get in my car I start chasin'
Is it when my mind goes blank when you look into my eyes
Is it like you or is love just a lie

I didn't grow up perfect
But I come from a good home
I learned to clean, cook and hold my own
I don't care about taking anything that's yours
I'd be good at making you happy and doing our chores

I wouldn't care if we lived in a one-bedroom apartment or somewhere on some land
I don't need a fancy car to drive that I can't understand
I'm pretty simple
I could ease your life
Let me make our bed
I wanna be called your wife

Love Is Missing Me

I go out and see couples nose to nose
I see them holding onto each other like it's life or death
Lost in each other's eyes, lost in each other's breath
If they have each other they probably believe they can survive on a dime
I'm out here still waiting on mine

Am I missing love or is love missing me
I run into it then I get set free
Am I missing love or is love missing me
Where are you Cupid
I keep falling for stupid
I ain't missing love, love is missing me
Love is missing me

Black and White

It's not the same
Oh how it used to be
Sometimes I cry when I hear your voice
It's not the same happiness, it's not the same joy
Something about it has been destroyed

Black and white
The difference between day and night
That's what you are
That's how you make me feel
You won't trust me but my lips are sealed
You're so black and white

Over Him

Even though you and I were no good it still made it hard to leave
You got me somewhere where I thought nobody could look at me,
that's what I believed
Then he did and I never looked away

I let you go
I never looked back
Sometimes it was hard, but little by little I got over you
But tell me,
how am I gonna get over him

The way you treated me
you basically handed me to him
And that's okay
Cause hey…

I let you go
I never looked back
Sometimes it was hard, but little by little I got over you
But tell me,
how am I gonna get over him

Hurt People, Wanna Hurt People

Standing on the outside
You won't let me in
Cause you've lost trust before and you don't wanna lose it again
I'm not like them and I'll say it again
I'm not going after you the way most girls go after men

I wanna love you if you'll let me
I wanna touch you
I know I can make you feel free
I know hurt people, wanna hurt people but that ain't me
Yeah hurt people, wanna hurt people

I wanna show you good is still here
And I won't leave you dead
You've let the poison from the past get to your head

If today I don't tell you the love I feel for you
I wonder if it would even make a difference if you ever knew
The days come and the days gone
This has been on my chest for so long
I can't get out the words because I'm scared

You, you don't know who I am
Let's be real you couldn't give a damn
We spend time
You never promised to be mine
You don't have a clue
Sit back and watch me baby
See what I do
I've been coming around and around
I promise I'm gonna make a name in this town

Dangerous To Kiss

You've got me speechless
I'm like so taken by your eyes
I can see the truth and some uncensored lies
I try to speak and nothing comes out of my mouth
You get me even more when I know what you're thinking about

You brush my hair away from my face
My heart skips a beat and starts to race
We start as two but feels like one
Your tongue is a drug, baby I'm gone
Don't you know you're so dangerous, dangerous to kiss

I'd cry every night on your chest because
I'd be the luckiest girl in the world to lay next to you
and call you mine over and over again

Mr. Perfect

It's like there was no one like him that exists
When I slept at night I dreamed about him
When I poured my coffee in the morning I thought about someday making him a cup
It's like my bones ached for him
Why him
Why is he special
Why is he Mr. Perfect in my eyes
Sometimes I wonder if he was too perfect for me to ever attain

Does she wear a leather jacket and skinny jeans
Or is she yoga pants and the kind who drinks her greens
Is she a late-night movie in bed with a glass of red wine
Or is she a black dress, red lips and a five star dine

Let Me In

Tell me that I'm pretty
But don't hold my hand
Look at me like I'm stupid when I say you don't understand
Move-in like you want me then hold open the door
Why do I always want this when I've been here before

Let me in baby
Let me in
Why does it always feel like you're the lottery I'm trying to win
Let me in

I forgot now this is a man's world
And me, ha I'm just another girl
Tell me that our lives are worlds apart
Tell me what I don't know
But don't we all have the same starving heart

Already Met Her

I know who you're looking for
But you won't open that door
Your one and only, a lifetime of true love
Oh you got a way of making a girl feel enough but not enough

Oh maybe you already met her
But oh I know
Maybe you're thinking you could do better than her
I know you want someone so good
Who's only bad with you
Oh maybe you already met her
But oh I know
Maybe you're thinking you could do better

You live in the clouds so high
You fly on cloud nine
You've seen many types
You say you ain't buying it but you're buying into the hype

Your Vibe

Some people we meet and say goodbye
Some people we love and never know why
Some people give all that they have, but sometimes some people aren't enough
Some come along maybe for a lesson or two
Yeah some, but not you

You're the feeling I can't ever quite describe
It ain't your smile or charm, it's your vibe
It ain't all the heads you turn when you walk into a place
It's the 'I want you' look that peaks through your face
It's your vibe, it's your vibe that gives this broken soul a little life

Sometimes I wear my heart on my sleeve
Sometimes I know the truth but it's not the truth I wanna believe
Some of us are looking for a little hope just to get by
Some of us wanna give up but because of people like you we try

You're the feeling I can't ever quite describe
It ain't your smile or charm, it's your vibe
It ain't all the heads you turn when you walk into a place
It's the 'I want you' look that peaks through your face
It's your vibe, it's your vibe that gives this broken soul a little life
Your presence is fresh air and helps me unwind
There's not many out there that are your kind
It's your vibe that makes me feel alive

Let's step outside tonight on the balcony
Most likely on the 30th floor
Lean me over with my hair hanging off the ledge

Waiting On a Heartbreak

We ain't ever gonna be together
Cause I just can't get you to see
That we aren't really worlds apart
I'm just like you
You're just like me
We just keep dancing around each other
You're keeping me on my toes
Oh it ain't fair but sometimes that's the way it goes

I'm waiting on a heartbreak
And I ain't afraid
I'm waiting on a heartbreak
Yeah you, you're a tough one to shake
Sitting here waiting on a break

It's the way you say hello that lets me
know where this night will go

I Like The Way

I like the way you open the door shirtless
I like the way you make my head spin
I'm already a mess
I like the way you know how this will tempt me
I like the way you set my world free
I like the way we always happen like a movie scene
I like the way we fall into the sheets so clean
I like the way
I like the way you want me

Classy, Classy Dirty

What's gotten into me
I don't know
I don't misbehave like this
Stop looking at me
I already want the kiss
Ya know I keep it classy, classy
Tonight I think I'm feeling a little dirty
I know it seems like I have no shame
You don't either, I guess we're feeling the same
So baby let's keep it
Classy, classy dirty

Hush Me

I have everything rehearsed in mind
When I walk into the room I start choking
Words are hard to find
I start needing air
Before I know it your hands are in my hair

When you touch me
You always know how to hush me
I never say stop cause you take me to the top
When you touch me
So go ahead hush me, hush me

It's like you always know what I wanna say
Before I do, you say you love my eyes
Are you telling me lies or just trying to get your way

When you touch me
You always know how to hush me
I never say stop cause you take me to the top
When you touch me
So go ahead hush me, hush me

Who Are You

Who are you
when you're out on the town
Are you the king looking for the crown
Do you do the things you do to me
Do you always watch your back or do you even care if they see
Do you ever let your walls down or build them twice
Are you the honest man they see or are they just honest lies
Do you take a heart, make it fall in love
I bet you pick them strong so they know to be tough
Do you let your ego get the best of your head
Do you cast a spell in every bed
Do you even know who you are
Or is it that easy, is it all a blur

Afraid

I'm sweet like honey
I don't bite
Everything hits me heavy
This heart of mine doesn't take anything light

Don't be afraid
Afraid to get close
I know you feel something
In your eyes, it shows

Baby, don't, don't be afraid

Too Fast

I said it's too bright
You go turn off the lights
Come back to me, kiss me one time
Clock is ticking, we're running outta time

It's always too soon
It's always too fast
I wanna keep you here
How do I make it last

You've always got one foot on the go
How do you make it happen
If we don't have a chance to grow

It's always too fast
always too fast

Tasting You

I never had an appetite for things that happen late at night after dark
Never got into it the way some do
Till I tasted you
I became someone I never knew
Maybe I like it more than I should
I'm not gonna lie if that's what you wanted
I'd do it every night, I would
I have fun
It's fun tasting you

Natural To Me

I like to kiss you
I like the taste of your tongue
I like you without any clothes on
I like the details on your face
I like when you get your fingers wrapped around my lace
I like going as far as I can
I've never been this high on a man
It's natural to me

Love Addicts

Isn't it funny we're both the same
We get each other, we don't have to explain
You taste so good all the way down
I don't act like this till you're around
I'm a good girl
I don't do this
With you, it's just the way it is
Are we love sick
Or is this a trick
I think you and I are just love addicts

Well hello nice to meet you I wanna show you a girl you've never met before

I've never had ecstasy but if I had to guess
I think it would feel like you and me
Drenched in sweat with our hearts beating out of our chest
Let our imagination handle the rest

He's the kinda man that makes you wanna start cooking dinner
and folding laundry, damn...
I've never felt that before! Is that love?

You never say forever, but how does forever sound

Sultry Gaze

Your hands the way they touch
I swear I couldn't get any more closer to love
The lows hurt but I can't get enough
Your sultry gaze
Your intoxicating way
You never need my permission
I'm on board with this mission
Cause you always get me
With your sultry gaze

Teach Me

I wanna know what it takes to love you
What it takes to have you
What sets your world on fire
Who you want in your life
The kinda woman you desire
Teach me who to be
Cause I have a wild feeling she's a lot like me
Teach me the things you want done your way
Teach me cause I wanna stay

Crazier and Crazier

I'm standing in the mirror naked
Sometimes I take pictures but I never send it
Nobody ever told me I'm beautiful like you
Darling, you've touched all my insecurities away
You make me feel crazier and crazier
For your love, your touch
Enough is never enough
You make me feel crazier and crazier
For you
Crazier and crazier, tonight
So if I hit send
Will you think I'm crazy tonight?

Drunk Lies

Drink that whiskey and come onto me
Do I look prettier
Baby can you see
Kiss me once
Kiss me twice
Tell me something good
Drunk lies
I'll fall for them like I do over and over again
You want me
You got me
The way you want me
Kiss me once
Kiss me twice
Tell me something good
Drunk lies

Call me silly, but I wonder how you eat your spaghetti

Make It To Breakfast

I've been waiting all day
Waiting for tonight
Who knows what'll happen
Into the night
I've been dreaming of feeling you
Just your lip on mine
Can we make it to breakfast or is that crossing the line
I've been putting on make-up to cover all my flaws
I do it for me just cause
I've been sipping on the cocktail just to kill time
Can we make it to breakfast or is that crossing the line

Wildflowers

The night wind blowing and this city is beamin with lights
this ain't your place and neither is mine
you're here
I'm here let's kill some time
you got me runnin like I'm in a field of weeds up to my thighs
I don't even wanna ask any questions I'll just believe in your lies
you got me in the palm of your hands
my petals are coming undone like wild…wildflowers tonight

Tantric

Never felt anything like your hands
I could try to tell you
you wouldn't understand
it's in your mysterious look
now I can't stop craving it
you got me on the hook
with every touch all the visuals
you've got a way that's unusual
it's so tantric
the room so static
my body wants your body
we feel it, it's magic, so tantric

We all deserve love
Real love
Not settled love
Not learned to love
But love
The kind where you want nothing but love

Grass is greener

Some think the grass is greener on the other side
So many options in this world so open wide
I keep watering where it may never grow
But I'll keep watering till you know that I'll water it forever
Forever to go
The grass is only greener where you stand
Maybe if I keep watering it someday, you'll want my hand
The grass is only greener on whatever side you stand

At first look, I fell in love with his humble confidence and free spirit

Begin Again

So many times, I wanted to give up the fight
Sitting here with you it's a new moon tonight
Look at us caught in each other's eyes
I don't think with us the magic or mystery ever lies
I was afraid to finish this story cause I never wanted it to end
But I think tonight somehow, we have begun again

Dream

Was it a dream?
You and me
You bring out what no-one has ever seen
This side of me that comes alive
Never wanna leave I just arrived
Was it a dream?
This fantasy
Why can I picture the future with you and me
Was it a dream?

Wings

I always knew I wanted someone that empowered me
Someone that triggered my emotions
Someone who could get ahold of me and control me
Someone who's passion I could feel
Someone like him
He is all of that
I'm not sure he knows the wings he's given me to fly

Enough

He is the sexiest thing I've ever set my eyes on
An addiction of the heart
The way he moves
The way he speaks
I can't get enough
When is enough just enough

Morning Dreams

Go to bed and I'm are staring at the ceiling
It's a happy but a heartache kinda feeling
Close my eyes and you're right there
I wanna wake you but I wouldn't ever dare
Wake up and I feel you on me
I wanna keep you here
I don't wanna open my eyes cause then I know you disappear

I know I can't have you all day
But I can have you right now
In my, in my morning dreams
It always goes so much faster in the moment
I wanna make this last forever long
You're in my head, a perfect poem that I've read
I wanna sleep and I just wanna stay in bed with you
Wake up and I feel you on me
I wanna keep you here
But If I look, you'll disappear
I know you disappear
I know I can't have you all day
But I can have you right now
In my, in my morning dreams
I just wanna keep on sleeping cause I know it's how I'm keeping you with me
In my, in my morning dreams

Piece of me

You let the whole world in with the stories you have to share
and there's something about that's rare
I know your heart must be full with
the little piece of everyone you keep
no matter where in the world you are tonight
I hope you're searching for a piece of me

In front of him, I always wore my biggest smile, a cute outfit and tried to be my best self. I wanted him to always see me that way. Not how I am when I go home crawl into my bed and miss him and cry.

Twin Flame

My world began to change the day we said hello
I was pretty young
every word would get stuck on my tongue
but I could feel the twin flame
you make my heart feel like it's on crack
when I see your body I'm ready to attack
soul to soul
we are the same
have you ever met your twin flame

I always enjoy getting ready before seeing him. It always feels like I'm 19 again. He always notices the little things that always elevates my confidence.

Oct 11

Things happen the way they should
sometimes I wonder if Oct 11 I knew
I'd show up late
I've asked myself many times
can't get it right without wine
nice to meet you and a handshake
friends warned me, but I wasn't pumping the breaks
I said I was gonna getcha no matter what it takes
you like the chase I could feel it
I was dreaming about that kiss ready to steal it
moving slow, but steady
still 19 and wasn't ready
so I stalled around
danced to the beat of the sounds
around and around, town to town

I know I love him. I think he sees it in my eyes. You know how you just look at someone and know? That's how I feel with him. I feel like time stands still, still, I look away

Redefine Beauty

I've been to some pretty places
I've seen some pretty blondes and rich faces
I've seen palm trees in L.A. and I've seen how the scenery of life can change by day

it's pretty when it's pretty
then when you tell me I've grown up to be who I am
you redefine beauty
the parts of me I can't see

from east coast to the west
you see me at my best
redefine my beauty
even when I'm acting pretty crazy
you ain't blind and somehow you show me what you find

He doesn't know it, but I do! We both want the same kind of love. A scared bond only two can feel, a love so deep only we can understand it, and mostly a heart that never gets tired of loving, forgiving and accepting cause we're all humans and we will all eventually mess things up. I know my heart would accept him with all his flaws and all. I already do!

Times Affair

It's a mind game
can't get ahead, you start falling behind
the whispers behind your back are
always there to remind
times a love affair
between you and I
make yourself a timeline but that timeline is a lie
they can call me a fool
but times a love affair
the greatest affair of this life
don't worry about me, honey we're all cheating time

When I look at him, I see a leader. Someone who I could follow forever.

Unfinished Letters

I've started them many times
words that don't come naturally that are hard to find
I've ripped them up thrown them away
cause I've wondered what's there even to say
I've written many over the years
over morning coffee or late night wine tears
I've found my excuses to never finish any
I've lost count
I've written so many

Most people won't get it, but it's hard to walk away from anything that gives you a thrill, gives life a purpose and makes you fall in love with yourself

Finding God

If you ever lose yourself in this world, have faith in him. It's interesting where you'll go for that last shred of hope. As time passes and we begin to see things differently, I believe we begin to lose faith in the people around us. We question what is and isn't real. God was never a question for me. I've always believed and had faith, but I think I'd become distracted over the years. I believe we all go through that stage in our lives. We all come full circle at some point. For me, it was a one-on-one battle with my heart. Something that no one close to me could possibly relate to or comprehend. It's easy for people to tell you what you need to do, but no one knows how difficult that is unless they're trying to climb that mountain themselves. There is nothing more terrifying and liberating than feeling isolated. I felt like I'd been losing the thing in life that had given me a deeper purpose, that had made me see life in a new light, and that had made me feel fearless in pursuing my dreams. It was that sense of helplessness that made me realize I needed to pray.

I used to be afraid of God because I was trying to avoid judgement, but once you've been judged by everyone, you realize God will always be there. Every day, I'd pray to God to make me into the person I needed to be in order to be seen. Make me the woman I required. Help me to be the person I know I am, but who I struggle to be when I am nervous, anxious, or scared. I believe I was pleading with God to help me grow and become stronger. The most important lesson I've taken away from this journey is that I knew I needed to change my ways. I had become so preoccupied with what I desired that I had forgotten to pray to God on occasion. To be honest, it's been a difficult journey. I'm still figuring things out and building this relationship with him, but I can tell you that if you have faith, he will heal your heartaches and get you through the day. I may get lost from time to time, but I will always believe and let him lead the way, and I still believe he will lead me to the fulfillment of my wildest dreams.

For The Most Part

I don't like to cry in front of people
It makes me feel weak
Even when tears start rolling I'll turn my cheek
For the most part, I'm strong
For the most part, I'm tough
For the most part, I hide it even when it's rough
For the most part
I don't like to share my heart cause who truly wants your best
They wanna get to you to see if you fall for it
Honey, it's all a test
For the most part, I'm strong
For the most part, I'm tough
For the most part, I hide it even when it's rough
For the most part
For the most part, I just wanna feel loved

Fearless

Afraid, I've been afraid of life and to live
I searched for my purpose but believed I had nothing to give
I looked left, I looked right
Even the moon didn't talk to me at night
There you've been my shining light
Holding the torch, being my guide
Through the pain and the sorrow
I wouldn't trade the minutes that I borrow
Cause this is goodnight
But tomorrow I'll wake up
Fearless

Keep Me

Don't you feel the longing I feel in my heart tonight
Do I have to say it or can I just hold you tight
When my shirt slips off my shoulder
The night starts getting colder
For once I wish you'd keep me
My heart is screaming don't leave me
As I walk out
Keep me
Keep me
Keep me in your heart

Words are Words

I wish I believed in promises
The way I called out lies
I wish I saw the actions instead of me always asking why
I wish I didn't believe in the saying talk is always cheap
Well I do cause I'm crying myself to sleep
I believe, words are words

Timeless

Do you believe in eternity
I do if there's you and me
There's no denying
We can hide our words but our bodies aren't lying
It's the way your fingertips send a shock to my heart
I get lost in you
If it's not love maybe it's art
You and I are timeless
It's time, it's time we confess

Should Be

It should be the way you drive me crazy waiting around
It should be the way my feet tingle when they feel the ground
It should be the way I spend days putting together what I wear
It should be the way I don't want to but I do care
It should be the way my heart races seeing your face
It should be how we go nowhere but through your eyes
I'm in a different place
It should be how my daydreams are my reality
I think now I know what it feels like
That's how love should be

Heartstrings

What they say could be true
There could be no me and you
I could be letting this youth slip
There's no tattoo like the one you leave on my lips
You got me by the heartstrings
Tell me it's a real thing
Help me prove to myself I'm worthy of love
Tell me I am enough
Don't play with my heartstrings
Tell me it's a real thing

Monday

I can't wait for a Monday where I open my eyes to your face
I can't wait for a Monday where we're in bed until noon
I can't wait for a Monday where we don't want it to be over so soon
I can't wait for a Monday where the smell of coffee is in the air
I can't wait for a Monday where your hands are in my hair
Today sucks, it's going slow
I know there will come a day
Where you're loving me like Sunday
I'll wanna wake up cause you're my Monday

3:49

It's hard to get to sleep
Sometimes the only way to find some peace is just to believe
3:49 I open my eyes when you finish dancing in corners of my mind
I see you how I always do underneath that spotlight
I thought tonight would be a good night and I could sleep tight
3:49 I open my eyes
It's 3:49 I wonder if you opened your eyes too

Just Like The Stars

Stars, there's a reason they are so far out in the sky
They only come out at night
To catch the eyes
That twinkling light
Leaving you in a daze
It'll disappear by morning
They never stay
Baby, you're just like the stars
So damn far
Just like the stars fading away
Just like the stars
you don't, you don't ever stay

Worth The Fight

Everyday from one hour to the next
I don't know what to do it's a nonstop battle in my head
This is my life and I wonder
Is it worth the fight
Fighting for someone who's gone when they're gone
I always show up with my favorite lipstick on
Putting miles on my tires
It's 2 am and I'm starting to feel tired
I feel like you're just fucking with me
I'll still put my best dress on
I'll entertain my dreams till you're gone
Cause it feels like it's worth the fight

When You're Mine

I wanna go to sleep
Don't wanna wake up
I hate the sun and the light on my face
I don't wanna feel anymore
I'm done looking for my place
I get why people take things to numb how they feel
I'm tired of faking the hurt that's so real
I'm tired of pretending that I'm okay
When in reality I don't know if I'm counting the hours or the days
So now I'm gonna go to bed with water flooding my eyes
I'll be okay, I'll believe in the lies
Just wake me when you're mine

Headspace

Palm trees or city lights
Ocean waves and moonlight
Friendly smiles or drunk nights
I can't get away, can't sway
From my headspace
Internally going psycho
I feel like I'm about to blow
You're the only place I wanna go
Night out, fancy dinner
Hearts aching, I'm a sinner
I can't get away, can't sway
From my headspace
Baby, I wanna runaway
Runaway from this headspace

I wanna fight for you
But it always feels like I'm just fighting with myself

Heart of a Man

I don't like this feeling
Going from happy to sad, sad to happy
Same damn cycle
These feelings recycle
I know I'm strong the way you got me
This feels wrong
Losing sight of reality
Aren't butterflies supposed to set you free
Lord give me, give me
The heart of a man
So I can wander through life without a plan
No sad tears at night when you've got the heart of a man
Ain't nobody you gotta understand
When you've got
The heart of a man

Take Me To a Restaurant

I've had the time of my life
Your lips locked in mine
Always running out of time
Till baby next time

But next time…
Take me to a restaurant
Cause that's what I really want
Maybe a cup of coffee
12am, back booth you and me
Take me to a restaurant

Why can't you understand
All I really wanna do is hold hands
We can drink some cheap wine
Talk till the sun shines

String

Diamonds… they sure catch eyes
People compare sizes, prices and tell sweet lies
They stand for love for what they believe
They still have their problems no matter what they have up their sleeves
We wait our whole life for this ring to make us feel complete
If I have you, you've already got the ring beat
I'll take a string if you ever wanna tie the knot
I don't need a rock to hold the spot

Suffocation

My hands are sweaty
My chest hurts
I remember this feeling
It feels like love
My toes tingle
I think I'm losing circulation
My body needs you
I need a vacation
My mouth can't talk in case I say the wrong thing
I could listen to you forever
Talk or sing
I sit in silence with all I want to say
I pray I'll have the nerve to spit it out someday

I built a wall between me and you
Cause I didn't think I could ever climb yours
Now I can't break mine
I wanna show you all my colors and who I am
I never thought it would be this hard
I don't know how to play this game, I'm mixing the cards
I wanna break your wall and crumble mine
I'm tired of boundaries
I wanna cross every single line
I wanna show you the woman in me

Heal me tonight
I'll cry tomorrow
Take me to my happy place
Make it slow
Heal me tonight
I'll cry tomorrow

I Wanna Know

What's your favorite color
How do you like your coffee made
Do you believe in true love or do you believe the magic always fades
Do you stick one foot out or wrap your feet in the sheets
Do you hold onto records or throw away your receipts
Do you like having breakfast for dinner on a Sunday night
Do you believe in being wrong or do you always have to be right
Do you hate doing laundry or old dishes
If I could grant them
What would be your three wishes
Do you like staying in bed a little longer to get extra morning kisses
Do you call your mama to say hello
These are the things I care about
The things I wanna know

Even if I lose, love will win, love always wins

I just always had a craving for a deep love. One
I can't explain to anyone but just feel. I've felt it in moments
but never long enough.

One Man To Another

I can't tell him
I'm gonna tell you
I feel kinda bad you've already bought me a drink or two
I shouldn't be confessing my love of one man to another
I can't help it but I'm not here to be your lover
I'm not gonna get weak or fall for you for the night
You're thinking if you listen to me ramble long enough
I just might
I shouldn't be confessing my love of one man to another
I can't help it but I'm not here to be your lover
And I ain't the kinda girl to go from one man to another

They Say

They say never hold back
Give all you have
Love who you love
You may only be lucky enough to get that love back
Even if you're lucky enough
The love may never be enough
We're told in this world to always do what our heart desires
But it's hard when you keep trying
You get tired
I'm having a hard time figuring out if it was ever meant for me
Cause I always go for the kinda love that can hurt me

Sexual Desire

You're more than a sexual desire
I want you to take me even higher
Emotionally and spiritually
There's more to me I want you to desire
Come take me higher and higher
I wanna be more than a sexual desire

Outta My System

I don't need a late-night drink at a bar
I don't need to be entertained by a stranger
I don't need to always feel the thrill
I got all of that outta my system
I can't get you outta my system

I've done all the things people don't talk about
I'm glad I did em, I got it out
I got all of that outta my system
I just can't get you outta my system

Asking God

Maybe you're asking God where she is
Maybe you're looking with a blind eye
I'm asking God where he is
I can feel this so deep it doesn't get better than this

Maybe he ain't giving you what you want
Maybe he ain't giving me what I want
Maybe he's trying to get us to see eye to eye

Look at us lost in the world going to bed with one side empty both probably asking him why

Maybe we need to make changes how we live
Maybe he needs to see before we can receive we're both willing to give

Woman Like Me

Rough around the edges
Never gives in
I'm the kinda woman who doesn't always have to win
Your words may leave a scar on my heart
I know it's just passion
I get it, it's the art

I know, I know, I know
A man like you
Needs a woman like me
Someone who doesn't tie him down
Still, lets him be a little gypsy
Baby, I'm telling you
I understand a man like you
The way you understand a woman like me

Meet You Again

How this started was so unpredictable
I knew you were mystical
You took my breath away
Still, now I stand not knowing what to say
I'm little more grown-up
I have a little more self-respect
I'm on my way to making something of myself
I don't kiss people just cause they wanna kiss me
I hold my value high
But I won't lie, if you ask me I wouldn't change a thing
If I met you for the first time all over again

7 Wonders

I've looked you deep in the eyes
I've felt the pull from your soul
I wonder if you feel me do you see the half or the whole

I've looked across the deep blue sea
I've wondered if this is what you mean when you're out there feeling free

I've drank my coffee with my hands shaking
thinking of your love
I've wondered if this is it or will I ever be enough

I've dreamed about you on long flights home
wondered about what a difference our days and night

I've seen my unborn babies in your eyes
is God showing me my life
I've wondered if they've all been lies

I've practiced saying my vows to you
in my dreams, I've seen us by the ocean saying I do

I think I've finally found my way around your mind
there are still some things I'm wondering that I can't find

My biggest fear in life is watching
the sunsets with the wrong man
telling him lies like I love you
and raising babies together
every night I pray it's you so
I don't have to pretend my whole life

Better You

It's the way you play the world
turning heads of every girl
they see only the outside of you
believing the goodness they read is all true
they only know the better you
they don't know how cold you are
when things get real you take it far
running off cause you can escape
if this is the real you
is the other you just a fake
the compliments that flood your feed
man they follow is oh so sweet
they'll never know what is true
cause they'll forever know the better you
I won't be the one to take away what they see
maybe they are right and it's just me

Just a face

The dark places you take me nobody knows
It's crazy, it's crazy, it's crazy
they say you're doing well, so we see
they don't know what's going on in me
it's a hurricane, it's insane and the pain
they see me going place to place
at the end of the day honey
this smile you see it's just a face

Flipping You

You told me once you keep playing the cards that life handed you
I got this deck that I've been shuffling for some time too
It's turning into a game that got me drunk on you and wine
I've been flipping these cards
Call me crazy, call me a diehard
Gods got me flipping you
I know these cards aren't handed to everybody
So if you're playing me, I don't mind playing you too
Cause I bet if God handed me a new deck
I'd still be flipping you

Valencia

He was a good one
Tried to love me but couldn't love me
I fell in love with a boy
And stayed in love with him
Till I met the man
When he kisses me
I knew that was God taking me away from him and
I had to walk with the plan
Though my heart aches that's how it had to be
I don't think I could've ever left him if he didn't kiss me
He was just the hope, the fancy that I chased
Til the night at the Valencia
I let myself go and walked out with grace

They're gonna laugh at me if I crash and burn
They're gonna clap their hands if I can't get up
They're gonna follow you and watch you closely
Forever and always
And probably ask me...hey did you see
They're probably gonna call me crazy
They're gonna say even if it happens it ain't gonna last
They're never gonna look past
They're probably always gonna think nobody else in my eyes will be
good enough
If I listened to them I wouldn't be where I am
So I'll always love with an open heart even if I fall apart

This Bottle

I wanna call you tonight
I don't dare cause I wanna spill my heart and I don't know if you'd care
So I don't reach for the phone
I reach for the bottle
I won't tell you how I'm feeling
I'll tell this bottle
The words I would probably stumble upon
I can write it on this bottle
This bottles with me when it gets dark
This bottle says 'hey have another' when I'm falling apart
This bottle helps me feel
The raw, the hurt, the real
When I can't reach you
I can always reach for this bottle

Dance Floor

I've never felt so free to be myself
When the lights are dim
The silence is the music
When your eyes make me lose it
When I watch you watch me
Baby your body is my dance floor
It's an escape, the way my heart beats
When the blood rushes from my feet
You are my dance floor
I love to watch you, watch me
Dancing on this dance floor

Know Me

I'm not one who thinks so highly of myself
I may not have the prettiest face but I have a pretty heart
I may not have a lot to bring to the table but I promise the table would never be empty
I can see us laughing on the floor
Listening to music that takes us back
Teaching each other a thing or two
Wish you'd get to know me
Cause baby, I know you I can take you back
To a time where we escape the world we're living in today
Cause we're both like that
Wish you'd get to me know me
Cause you don't know me like that

Blind

When I first saw you
I couldn't see
I introduced myself and let it be
I saw your eyes scan me as I walked through those barn doors
My heart was somewhere else fighting another war
We all walk into it blindly
We wouldn't walk in if we could see
The love, the electricity, the mystery
I fell into it
Oh honey I still can't see
I'm walking blindly

View

From one state line to another
Oh life looks different in a blink of an eye
From the dirt roads to the city lights
From not listening to you and putting up a fight
Isn't life great I'm staring out the next window looking out at the view
All cause, I've been betting it all on you
What a view
I wouldn't need anything else in life
I could spend rest of my life just looking at you

I'm Scared

I'm scared
Scared of the pain I feel
It seems so dark that most days I can't seem to find the light
The perception people have of your life doesn't matter
It's a funny thing about humans
Nobody ever cares until something tragic happens
I don't care for anyone to care
I just want this pain to go away
I just want to be able to take a full breath

Book On A Shelf

I don't wanna be a burden to him
With all these feelings and pain
If he knew my every thought he'd think I'm insane
I fill up these pages with everything my heart has to say

Worship

I've lost my faith here and there
I've found myself in my single hearts affairs
I see you, I see gold
Someone to follow, someone to hold
The body I could worship and the language I can speak
The hands that make me tired
The chase that keeps me weak
When I lose my faith in him
I turn to you
This is something I've never told you
But it has been true
If I ever lose him, I need you

I've changed so much for him
I've lost people in my life
I've been judged
I feel weak
I've put my body through so much
The pain triggered a part of me I thought I wouldn't have
to meet again
In less than 24 hours I met her again
I pray to God
Believing is hard these days

Love Bible

Having respect for someone at the end of the day. You have to give respect to earn respect. It's as simple as it sounds, but it seems it takes time to learn. You can't force respect though. Only if the person is respectable can you give them that.

I know now that I want to be the kind of woman who brings peace to a situation. When things are intense and heated...I always want to be the peacemaker.

Being attracted to someone who can lead you is not control. If they make you want to be a better being, fulfill your wildest dreams, and help you grow. I could follow that forever.

You can't talk badly about someone you want to keep in your life. There will be bad days...lots of them. Goes back to the root of the relationship and how much respect you have for them.

Be the person you want them to be to you. Sometimes we so badly want to see change/action from others we forget about ourselves. Take a step back, look in the mirror, and ask yourself "Am I the best version of me?" So often we want others to change, sometimes if we just tweak a few things within ourselves things change for the better naturally.

"She wanted the world"

"The world was him"

www.ingramcontent.com/pod-product-compliance
Lightning Source LLC
LaVergne TN
LVHW040143080526
838202LV00042B/3013